First published in 2020
by Jessica Kingsley Publishers
73 Collier Street
London N1 9BE, UK
and
400 Market Street, Suite 400
Philadelphia, PA 19106, USA

www.jkp.com

Library of Congress Cataloging in Publication Data
A CIP catalog record for this book is available from the Library of Congress

British Library Cataloguing in Publication Data
A CIP catalogue record for this book is available from the British Library

ISBN 978 1 78775 221 4
eISBN 978 1 78775 222 1

Printed and bound in China

MY DAD THINKS I'M A BOY?!

A Trans Positive Children's Book

Sophie Labelle

Jessica Kingsley Publishers
London and Philadelphia

Hi! My name is Stephie. I'm 7 years old.

I like bugs, *Ninja Dog*, and all sorts of books.

The thing I like the most is watching **horror movies** late at night.

My favorite thing to eat is **spaghetti**.

I like every kind of pasta and I could have spaghetti for every meal.

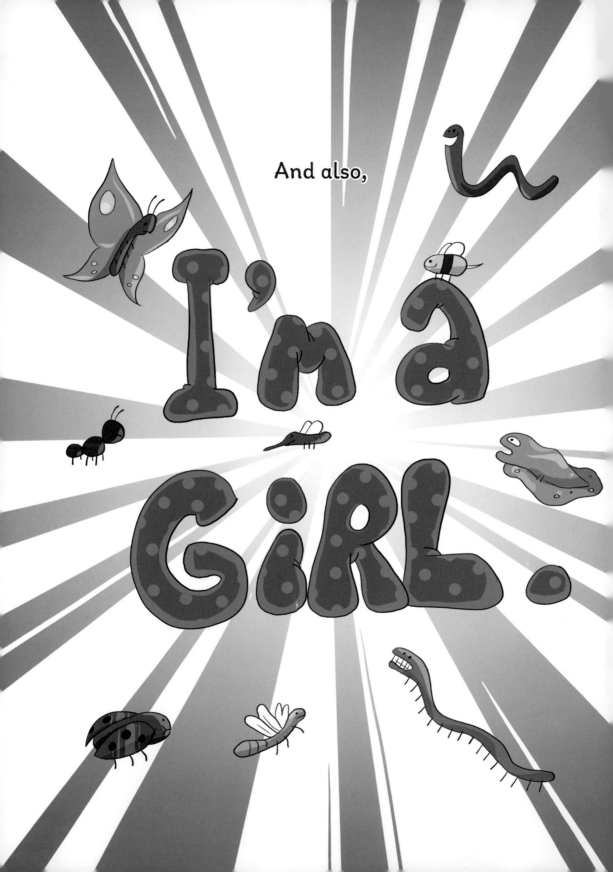

And also,

I'm a
GiRL.

You'd think that's pretty easy
to understand, right?

My dad thinks
I'm a boy named

STEPHEN

who likes wrestling
and fishing.

But that's what
my dad likes.

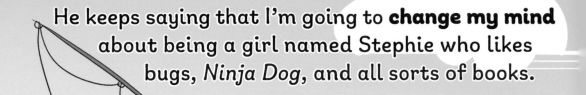

He keeps saying that I'm going to **change my mind** about being a girl named Stephie who likes bugs, *Ninja Dog*, and all sorts of books.

He's a very **stubborn** adult.

I think it's because when I was born, the doctor was a bit **confused** and thought I was a boy since my body looked like many boys' bodies.

Uh...it's a **boy**? I guess?
But not everybody looks **the same**!
Doctors are also adults.
They can't always be right.

So, my parents raised me as a boy named Stephen until I could talk and tell them they were **all wrong**.

My mom understood pretty quickly. She started to call me Stephie...

...but my dad still doesn't get it.

Whenever I go to visit his house, I know he's gonna say that I'm his **son** and keep calling me by my **old name.**

I try to be patient with him.

It can be hard for adults sometimes.

I agree to go fishing with him and try to look like I'm having fun, even though **I really don't like it.**

He wants me to put worms on my hook, but I like them!

"Help me!"

We go to see wrestling matches together because he wants to do "father-and-son" activities.

I don't like it, but whatever makes him happy.

...but then my dad threw such a **tantrum** at the store that I agreed to go as a **superhero** just so he would calm down.

On Halloween night, there was an older lady who was so happy to see a girl dressed as a superhero; she said that girls should be able to dress as

whatever they want.

I told her I didn't actually want to go as a superhero, it was just to make my dad happy.

She was a bit confused but still gave me a huge pile of my favorite chocolate bars.

It was probably because she thought I was being so kind to my dad.

My mom thinks it's because my dad feels like his son named Stephen **died** when I told them I was actually their daughter.

Adults often think they can decide who children should be.

But that's not how it works!

No one **except me** gets to decide who I am.

And sometimes it's hard, because people won't see you as who you are, even when you tell them.

It hurts when my dad doesn't see me as myself, because I love my dad and I don't want to be angry at him.

He's the daddiest dad I've ever had.

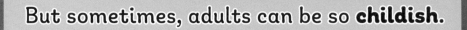

But sometimes, adults can be so **childish.**

Questions for further discussion

In the book, Stephie's dad believes that his daughter is someone that she isn't: he thinks that she likes wrestling and fishing, and that she is a boy.

* Why do you think that happens?

* Does your parent do this too sometimes?

Stephie is transgender, which means that people thought she was a different gender when she was born. You can't know a person is transgender unless they tell you, and it makes it hard to know for sure how many transgender people there are.

* Do you know other books with transgender characters?

* Do you think there are enough books with transgender characters, and why?

Many trans people won't want you to know they are transgender for several different reasons; for example, because they're scared people might judge them or treat them differently if they knew.

* What is something you can do to make sure your transgender friends and classmates feel welcomed and safe?
  - What is something your class can do?
  - What is something your school can do?

Being of a certain gender doesn't necessarily mean you like everything stereotypically associated with that gender. Stereotypes are beliefs and ideas about a group of people that are largely widespread.

* Do you know any examples of gender stereotypes?

* Did you ever stop doing something because of stereotypes?
  - How did that make you feel?

* What is something you can do to fight against stereotypes?

In our society, we attribute a gender to all sorts of things that don't need one. Toys, emotions, jobs, clothes, or colors are often labeled as being gendered, but they are actually for everyone.

Toys: Can you name some toys that are gendered? Do you think there's any reason some people can't play with them because of their gender?

Emotions: Humans all have the same range of emotions, but some emotions are considered typically masculine or typically feminine. Can you name a few? How do you think it makes people feel, when they're not allowed to express their emotions because of their gender?

Jobs: It can be really hard to have a job that is heavily gendered if you're not the gender stereotype associated with that job. What jobs are considered for girls? What jobs are considered for boys? Why is it important to make it so that everyone can do the job they like?

Clothes: Clothes are objects: they don't have a gender. Wearing a tie doesn't make you a boy and wearing a dress doesn't make you a girl. What are some reasons why you would choose to wear a certain article of clothing? (For example, comfort, weather, activity, etc.)

Colors: Some years ago, pink was for boys and blue was for girls. The ideas we associate with each color changes over time, and they don't mean the same things for different people. Is there any reason why colors should have a gender?

> Transgender, non-binary, or gender non-conforming students might feel overwhelmed by these discussions or questions. Be mindful not to single them out and respect their need for privacy!

Further Reading

From the Stars in the Sky to the Fish in the Sea (Kai Cheng Thom)

George (Alex Gino)

Phoenix Goes to School (Phoenix and Michelle Finch)

Are You a Boy or Are You a Girl? (Sarah Savage and Fox Fisher)

More books and resources by the same author can be found at www.serioustransvibes.com

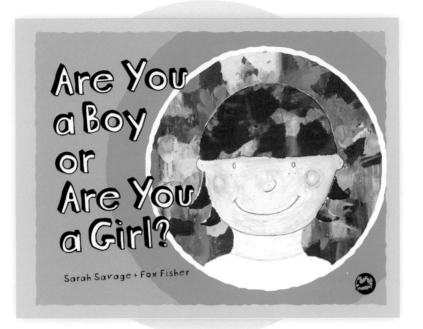

Are You a Boy or Are You a Girl?

Sarah Savage and Fox Fisher
Illustrated by Fox Fisher

Hardback · ISBN 978 1 78592 267 1 · eISBN 978 1 78450 556 1

Tiny prefers not to tell other children whether they are a boy or a girl. Tiny also loves to play fancy dress, sometimes as a fairy and sometimes as a knight in shining armor. While Tiny's family don't seem to mind, when Tiny starts a new school some of their new classmates struggle to understand.

"When a child selects a book and sees someone like themselves within its pages, they know they are not alone. It is a seemingly small gesture to us grownups, that enables a child to feel safe and secure. This breezy and beautifully illustrated book describes gender in playful, innocent terms, allowing children the space to discover themselves and to explore their surroundings joyfully. A must for any library."

Juno Roche, writer and campaigner

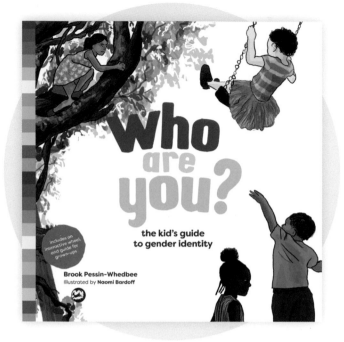

Who Are You?

The Kid's Guide to Gender Identity

Brook Pessin-Whedbee
Illustrated by Naomi Bardoff

Hardback · ISBN 978 1 78592 728 7 · eISBN 978 1 78450 580 6

This book introduces children to gender as a spectrum and shows how people can bend and break the gender binary and stereotypes. It includes an interactive wheel, clearly showing the difference between our body, expression and identity, and is an effective tool to help children 5+ understand and celebrate diversity.

"A much-needed non-fiction children's book exploring gender. *Who Are You?* will benefit every child!"

Pamela Wool, Director of Family Services, Gender Spectrum

Phoenix Goes to School

A Story to Support Transgender and Gender Diverse Children

Michelle and Phoenix Finch
Illustrated by Sharon Davey

Hardback · ISBN 978 1 78592 821 5 · eISBN 978 1 78450 924 8

Phoenix wants to wear her favorite purple dress to express her gender, but she is scared of being bullied on her first day of school. Follow Phoenix's journey as she arrives at school, makes some friends, stands up for herself, and helps us learn to be true to who we really are.

"Someday we'll live in a world where any child can wear a dress with freedom and delight, but until then, *Phoenix Goes to School* is a brilliant must-read for every child who either is a gender creative or transgender child or who wants to be their ally."

Diane Ehrensaft, PhD, Director of Mental Health, Child and Adolescent Gender Center, and author